Day
of the
Blizzard

Day of the Blizzard

by
Marietta Moskin

Drawings by Stephen Gammell

Cover by Paul Bachem

SCHOLASTIC INC.
New York Toronto London Auckland Sydney

ISBN 0-590-30092-X

Text copyright © 1978 by Marietta Moskin. Illustrations copyright © 1978 by Stephen Gammell. All rights reserved. Published by Scholastic, Inc., 555 Broadway, New York, New York, 10012, by arrangement with The Putnam & Grosset Group.

12 11 10 9 8   9/9 0 1 2/0

Printed in the U.S.A.   40
First Scholastic printing, March 1997

*For Jean Fritz,
with appreciation for the things
I learned from her.*

ONE

Katie turned down the kerosene lamp. Mama was asleep at last. Her breathing was coming easier and her face wasn't quite so flushed. Katie tucked in the sheets and carried the washbasin to the slop jar under the washstand. She glanced at the old clock on the mantel. Eleven o'clock! She must have sat on that bed for hours, putting cold cloths on Mama's burning forehead. Eleven o'clock . . . and Papa still wasn't home.

Where was Papa? His train had been due at Grand Central Depot at seven fifteen. Papa was a conductor on the New York Central Railroad. He had left New York City yesterday morning for his regular run to Buffalo. He should have been home hours ago. What was keeping him now?

The calendar on the wall had Papa's workdays marked clearly in his bold script. Yes, he *was* due in tonight: Sunday, March 11. That was today. But today was nearly over.

Katie reached for the calendar page, as if touching the words he had written would somehow bring Papa close. She idly traced the large 1888 at the top of the page with her finger. Had Papa said anything about coming home late? She couldn't recall.

Before he had left, Papa had grumbled about working a weekend shift. He didn't even know that Mama's fever had taken a turn for the worse. If he had known, he would surely have hurried home. He wouldn't leave Katie alone, trying to take care of Mama and the five-year-old twins.

Katie sighed. Usually she liked to do difficult, grown-up things by herself. Ever since she had turned twelve, Katie felt very grown-up. She was pleased when Mama depended on her. And Mama did.

"Dependable Kate," Mama called her, and Katie would flush with pride.

Right now, though, Katie wished for some help. It was scary, seeing Mama so weak. If only Aunt Maggie were here. Aunt Maggie was Mama's sister. She was smart and cheerful and she always made Katie feel good. But Aunt Maggie worked as a maid in a downtown hotel. There was no way to fetch her. So with Papa away, Katie was on her own.

She looked up at her parents' wedding picture in its heavy carved frame on the wall. There they both were: Papa stiff in his dark suit, staring into the camera; Mama, round-faced and smiling above the high lace collar held at the throat with a bow-shaped pin. Katie knew the pin. It was the special garnet brooch which Grandma Kate had brought all the way from Ireland. All the women in Mama's family had worn that pin on their wedding day. That's me too, Katie thought. Someday.

The twins were soundly asleep in the next

room. Katie wished that she too could stretch out on her cot. Eleven o'clock was way past her bedtime.

She turned to the window and leaned her forehead against the cold panes of glass. Outside it was raining hard. It had been raining all afternoon, but now it seemed worse than before.

Katie tried to open the window a crack, but the wind was stronger than she. What a storm! Yesterday it had been like spring. And now it was freezing cold. The storm played with the rain, lashing it against the windows, whipping it across the sidewalks, turning it into hailstones and needlelike chips of sleet.

In the pale circle of light shed by the streetlamp at the corner, Katie watched a man making his way along East Eighty-first Street. Katie wished it were Papa. The man was fighting his way against the storm, holding on to the lamppost, to the tree in front of the next building, to the garbage can at the curb. With each step his feet were sliding away under him, as if he were skating on ice. He *was* walking on ice! The pavement had become one giant sheet of ice, stretching across town.

Suddenly the man lurched crazily, his arms flailing the air. Katie nearly giggled out loud. He looked so funny, working so hard to walk just a few feet. Then she recognized him. It was Mr. Reilly, their downstairs neighbor. Mr. Reilly worked for the railroad too. He probably was just coming home from work. Perhaps he would know about Papa.

Katie tiptoed through Mama's room, past the sleeping twins, and through the kitchen to the front door. She ran down the three flights of stairs to the downstairs hall. She tugged at the heavy entrance door. Mr. Reilly was outside, climbing the front steps on his hands and knees. When he saw Katie, he held out his hand and she helped pull him up the last step.

Mr. Reilly took off his sopping-wet coat. He stamped his feet and blew into his hands. Icicles glistened in his dark beard.

"What a night!" he gasped. "Never saw worse in my life. Cold enough to freeze one's

ears off!" Mr. Reilly began to rub his left ear, which was a chalky white. After a moment it turned a fiery red. So did the tip of his nose.

Katie waited until Mr. Reilly had caught his breath. Then she tugged at his sleeve.

"Please, Mr. Reilly, have you seen Papa? He hasn't come home yet. Mama is sick, and I've been waiting and waiting. . . ."

Mr. Reilly seemed to really notice Katie for the first time. "Why, Katie!" he said. "No, I haven't seen your father all day." He shook his head. "If he was on an incoming train, I doubt that he'll make it home tonight. There's been trouble up and down all the lines. Icy rails, frozen switches, snowdrifts upstate . . . only a few trains made it into the depot tonight. And I heard tell there is more bad weather to come. It's bad enough as it is. Took me near on an hour to walk those few blocks from the Third Avenue El! Streets slick with ice. And the wind something fierce. I thought I might not make it—strong as I am."

Still shaking his head, Mr. Reilly began to climb the steep stairs to his second-floor flat.

Halfway up he looked back. "Don't worry, lassie," he said. "Your Pa will turn up. He knows how to take care of himself."

Katie slowly followed Mr. Reilly up the stairs. She heard him knock at his door, Mrs. Reilly's voice, and then the door closing behind the two of them. She felt so alone. Papa wasn't coming tonight. There was no one to look after Mama and the twins but Katie herself. And Katie was scared.

Mama had turned over in bed. She was moaning softly, but she was still asleep. So were the twins. Katie took off her shoes and lay down on Papa's side of the big bed. She'd have to stay in here in case Mama needed her during the night. It felt good to stretch out.

Tomorrow Mama will be better, Katie thought. She has to be. Everything will be better. Papa will come home and he'll know what to do.

Behind the heavy drapes, pellets of sleet were drumming against the windows. Gale winds made the panes rattle inside the sashes. The storm was growing worse.

TWO

"Snow! Katie, wake up. It's snowing outside!"

Michael, the taller of the twins, stood by the bed, pulling on Katie's arm. Behind him, Kevin was jumping up and down with excitement.

Katie sat up. She had fallen asleep in her clothes where she had stretched out on Papa's side of the bed. She felt stiff and cold. Michael had pulled the heavy drapes aside but only a little gray light showed through the stiff net curtains.

"Hush, you'll wake Mama," Katie whispered. She slid off the bed and went to look out the window. At first she couldn't see anything at all. A frosty garden of ice blossoms had grown across every windowpane. It took a lot of blowing and scraping to open up a tiny peephole. Even then she had to stand on tiptoe to see over the mound of fluffy snow piled high on the window ledge outside. Beyond that barrier, snowflakes were falling so thickly that they hid the other side of the street.

"Katie, can we go outside to make a snowman?" Michael begged. "Can we go slide in the snow?"

"Ssh, it's too early. It's still dark outside. Go back to bed," Katie whispered again. She glanced uneasily at Mama. But Mama was stirring. She opened her eyes.

"Is it morning?" she mumbled.

"It's scarcely five," Katie said.

Mama lifted herself up on one elbow. She looked around the room. "Where is your Pa?" she whispered. Her voice was so weak, Katie could hardly make out the words. Mama didn't wait for an answer.

"Tell Papa he must go for the brooch today.

16

He mustn't forget," she said. "The money and the ticket are in that envelope on the mantel. . . . Tell him now, Katie. . . . Give it to him. . . ."

The brooch! With all her worrying about Mama, Katie had almost forgotten. She stared at the stiff white envelope propped up against the mirror. The small green pawn ticket inside was all Mama had left of the bow-shaped garnet pin she'd worn on her wedding day.

Katie could hardly bear thinking about it. The glittering little bow was locked away in the strongbox of the Gotham Pawnshop, way downtown on Forty-fourth Street. It had been there ever since that awful day in December when both twins had been so sick with scarlet fever that Mama didn't think they would live. The $8.50 the pawnbroker gave her had paid for the doctor and costly medicines.

Mama tried to say more, but the effort was too much. She started to cough, the hard, hacking cough that had plagued her for so many days. She sank back onto her pillow and closed her eyes.

Katie was relieved that Mama didn't seem

to expect an answer. How could she tell her that Papa hadn't come home? Thinking of Papa brought a lump to Katie's throat. If only she knew what was happening to him. Mr. Reilly had told her that Papa would be all right, but . . .

Katie pushed her worries about Papa to the back of her mind. There was so much to do. Overnight, the icy air from outside had crept into the room. Katie shivered in her crumpled chambray dress. She stirred the ashes in the fireplace, but the fire had gone out. There were only a few lumps of coal left in the scuttle. If Papa had come home last night, he would have brought up more from the cellar. Katie threw what she had on the grate and put a match to the kindling. Mama needed warmth.

At the washstand, a thin layer of ice had formed on the water in the tall china pitcher. Katie carried it into the kitchen. The coals in the black kitchen stove were still alive. Katie fanned them into a blaze and filled the big iron kettle. Hot tea, water for washing, a pot set to boil for the breakfast stirabout . . . Katie had helped Mama so often to get the household started in the morning, she did it almost without thinking.

Instead her mind kept going back to the small green ticket inside the envelope in Mama's room. Katie knew why Mama was so worried about it. The loan had come due. Today was the last day for Mama to redeem her ticket—to go to the shop and get back the brooch. After today, the pawnbroker was free to sell the brooch to any customer—most likely for much more than the ten dollars Mama owed him.

Ten dollars! That was an awful lot of money. For ten dollars Mama could buy the new winter coat she needed so badly, or make half a dozen new dresses for Katie. Ten dollars would buy enough coal to heat all of their rooms for a whole winter and more.

But Mama had saved the money. She had worked late hours as a seamstress to earn extra money until all the quarters and dimes and nickels added up right. A lot of hems were taken up and shirtwaists taken in to get all that money together. Katie could almost see the piles of skirts, the mounds of coats and dresses Mama had worked on for all these months. So many extra stitches to lay ten dollars by. Now the large dollar bills and the green pawn ticket were safely sealed in their envelope, ready to be taken to the pawnshop today.

All of yesterday Mama had worried in the midst of her feverish dreams about that brooch. Dozens of times she had begged Katie to remind Papa of the errand—to make sure that Papa wouldn't forget.

"Don't worry, Mama," Katie had promised each time. "Don't worry, it will be all right."

But it wasn't all right. Papa wasn't home to keep Katie's promise.

Katie suddenly decided. "I'll just have to go myself."

It wasn't so hard to go to a pawnshop. She knew just where it was—the address was right on the envelope: Mr. Harry Lemmon, Gotham Pawnshop, 743 Third Avenue. That was near Forty-fourth Street, Mama had said.

The problem was Mama. Could Katie leave her alone with the twins? But the errand wouldn't take long if Katie went downtown on the Second Avenue El. The elevated railroads were much faster than the old-fashioned horsecars. And if she hurried, she could still make it before the fare went up from a half dime to a dime at seven o'clock.

From her own small hoard under her bed Katie took the round leather change purse Aunt Maggie had given her and shook some coins into the palm of her hand. A couple of three-cent pieces, two tiny half dimes, and one shiny dime. Plenty to take her downtown by El and back on the cheaper horsecars. With some luck, she might even be home again before Mama woke up. If only it would stop snowing. Snow always slowed up everything!

She took the envelope from the mantel and tucked it into the deep pocket of her coat. The money went into her other pocket. There, now all was safe. If only the twins could be trusted to behave themselves for a while.

Michael and Kevin were eating oatmeal at the kitchen table.

"I must run an errand for Mama," Katie explained. "Be good and look after Mama. If you need help, call Mrs. Reilly. I'll be back soon."

Katie paused on the second-floor landing. Should she tell Mrs. Reilly that she was leaving Mama alone with the twins? No. Mrs. Reilly was always so nosy. She'd want to know what her errand was and ask a million other questions. Katie was sure that Mama wouldn't like Mrs. Reilly to know about the Gotham Pawnshop.

Katie buttoned her coat to her chin and pulled on the gloves Mama had knitted for her last Christmas. She had borrowed Mama's warm mohair shawl and she wrapped it securely around her head and shoulders. Now she felt quite prepared for the storm, but when she opened the outside door, the wind hit her so hard that it almost spun her around. Icy snow sprayed into her face. The six steps of the stoop were nearly hidden inside a

mound of snow. For one silly moment Katie wished she'd brought down the twins' sled to slide down the steep incline.

How quiet it was on the street! Not a footstep or hoofbeat sounded, not a rattling of wheels against cobblestones. Nothing but the howling of the wind as it screamed through the block, tearing at anything not fastened down.

Mounds of white, wherever she looked. It *was* bad. But it's only snow, Katie thought. She pulled Mama's shawl closer around her head and plunged into the storm.

THREE

Katie had never seen snow like this. The thick flakes clung to her lashes so that she could hardly see. Somehow they slipped down her neck into the collar of her coat in spite of the mohair shawl. At least the wind was at her back. The strong gusts pushed her forward like an unseen hand.

In front of the next house a man was trying to clear the sidewalk with a shovel. But the swirling snow covered the ground almost as fast as he could dig. The man cursed out loud. Then he gave up. Slamming the shovel against the stoop, he stomped into the house.

Katie wondered if she should give up too. Would Mama have let her go out in this storm if she hadn't been sick? Probably not. Maybe the errand could wait until tomorrow. Maybe Papa would come home and do it himself.

But what if the brooch had been sold by tomorrow? How sad Mama would be. I promised Mama, Katie thought. Promises must be kept. And after all, it's only snow.

She plodded on. Across the street, two boys were trying to throw snowballs at each other. The powdery snow wouldn't stick, but they kept at it anyway. They seemed to be having a wonderful time.

Katie's fingers itched to start making snowballs too. Half of her longed to run across the street to join those boys in their fun. The other half remembered her errand. Not just for Mama—for Katie, too. Someday *she'd* want to wear that brooch—when she was old enough.

The boys had noticed Katie and were waving at her. One of them jumped right into the middle of a snowdrift. The snow reached to the top of his tall rubber boots.

Boots! That's what I need, Katie thought. She looked sadly down at her own scuffed high-button shoes. The leather was marked by dark, wet patches already, and her toes felt numb.

Only another block, Katie thought. I'll get warm on the train.

At the corner, the wind caught her so hard again that it nearly blew her right off the sidewalk. For a moment she couldn't breathe. Perhaps she shouldn't go on. But now the tall structure of the elevated railroad loomed up out of the snowy mist. Head down, Katie joined the stream of people surging toward the iron stairs.

The steps were slippery with ice and Katie's fingers were almost too stiff to cling to the iron railing in spite of her woollen gloves. On top she fumbled for her half dime to buy her ticket. The crowd carried her past the ticket taker onto the platform itself.

The ladies' waiting room was crowded. Women clustered around the pot-bellied stove in the corner. A steamy smell of drying wool and smoke and wet leather hung over the place. But at least it was warm. Katie leaned against the wall and waited for the tingling in her fingers and toes to stop. All around her, people were grumbling about the long delay of the trains.

Katie looked at the big station clock. Like all the other people, she was in a hurry too. She had left Mama alone with the twins. She hoped the train would come soon.

But when the steam engine huffed its way into the station about ten minutes later, the pale-green carriages behind it were jam-packed with people. It was hard to believe that anyone else could still get on. Again Katie let the crowd carry her forward. By herself she would never have made it, but a big, heavy man gave her a push through the door before shoving his way into the carriage behind her. For once, being small and thin was an advantage. Katie wormed her way into the middle of the coach. A kindly woman moved over a little so that Katie could perch on the corner of the wooden seat next to her. From here she could even look out of the steamed-up window a little. Katie began to enjoy herself.

The train moved slowly. It stopped often to let the conductor clear drifts of snow from the track ahead. The tracks ran at the second-story level of the buildings along its path. Leaning across her kind neighbor, Katie used her sleeve to wipe some of the steam off the window. Now she could look right into the windows of the people living on Second Avenue. From some windows, people looked right back at Katie. She wondered what it would be like to have trains passing so nearby a hundred times or more each day. Even where she lived, half a block away from the train tracks, the rumbling sound of the passing trains could be heard clearly all day and all night.

Each time the train stopped at a station, more people tried to crowd on. Only a few got off. Katie began to worry about the envelope in her pocket. So many people all around her! Papa had often warned her about pickpockets in a crowd. Just to be safe, Katie kept her hand in her right-hand pocket. The sharp edge of the stiff white envelope felt reassuring against her palm.

The train pulled out of the Fiftieth Street station. Only eight more blocks to the next station, Katie thought. Soon she'd be at the pawnshop with the ticket and the money. Soon Mama's brooch would be safe in her possession.

Suddenly the train's whistle sounded very loud. The train stopped with a lurch. The people standing in the aisles tumbled about. A fat lady almost landed in Katie's lap.

"What happened?" people asked each other. Nobody knew the answer. The train had stopped between stations. Outside, the snow kept falling from the sky.

"Where are we?" somebody asked.

"At Forty-eighth Street," somebody answered.

"Where is the conductor? What's going on?"

The conductor came into the car, followed by a rush of cold air. "Sorry folks," he said. "We're stuck. The train in front of us broke down. And the snow is piling up on the tracks too quickly. We can't go forward and we can't go back. You'll all have to be patient. We'll be here for a while."

FOUR

It was frightening being trapped so high above the street. To Katie, the railroad carriage suddenly became a crowded prison on wheels. Some people tried to leave the train and to walk back to the last station on the catwalk along the track. But the wooden planks were slippery, there was no guardrail, and the wind was blowing hard. Most of the passengers thought it was safer to stay right where they were on the train. As much as she wanted to leave, Katie thought so too. The stove at the end of the car kept the place snug and warm. Almost too warm, with so many people.

For a while, everyone was in a good mood. Even to Katie it began to seem like quite an adventure. All around her, people were talking to each other as if they were all old friends. But as time ticked away, many of the passengers became impatient.

"I'll be late for work," someone said.

"Why can't they clear the track?" someone else grumbled.

"They should get us down from here," a woman complained.

A man opened one of the train windows. "Help us," he shouted at the people watching from the buildings next to the track. "Hey, you in there—can't you help us get down?"

Suddenly a boy's head appeared over the side of the track.

"Over here, people," he shouted. "Want to get down? I've got a ladder. Five cents to use my ladder. I'll help you down."

Passengers began to scramble for the exits at each end of the carriage.

"Come on, let's get off," the woman next to Katie said. "I don't want to stay up here for another minute. I don't think it's safe."

Katie didn't want to stay either. But five cents! That was a lot of money. It was more than her fare to go home. But there was no choice. She had to get off. Mama was sick and home alone with the twins.

She climbed down the high steps of the railroad car to the slippery catwalk below. There were more ladders along the track now. And their owners were raking in the money. Everybody wanted to be first. Some people swung easily onto the shaky ladders. Others backed off in fear. There was a lot of screaming and squealing. Katie clung to the side of the railroad car. There was so much pushing and shoving. What if someone pushed her right off the track?

Now it was her turn. Katie dug her half dime out of her pocket. But when she held it out to the boy, he shook his head.

"No, you're just a girl," he said. "I don't take money from children. Come on, I'll get you down."

He helped Katie over the edge. It was a long, steep way down. Katie could feel the ladder swaying. The wooden rungs creaked

with each step. Her feet kept getting tangled in her skirts. But at last there was solid ground under her feet. Under the covering of snow she could feel the solid cobblestones of Second Avenue.

Now she would have to walk. She'd walk along under the elevated tracks. At least they gave a little shelter from all that snow.

She pulled her shawl closer around her and shoved her hands into her pockets. Something felt wrong. Something was missing. Where was her envelope?

Katie froze. Her heart skipped a beat. She pushed her hand deeper into her pocket—but the envelope still wasn't there. It wasn't in the other pocket either. It wasn't in the pocket of her dress. Katie searched all three pockets again. She found a crumpled handkerchief in one, her change and a paper-wrapped sour ball in another. But no envelope of any kind.

But that can't be, Katie thought. I can't have lost it. I was so careful. I held on to it all the time.

But had she? She had used both hands to

climb down from the track. It could have fallen from her pocket then.

Katie ran back to the ladder. People were still climbing down from the train. The snow at the foot of the ladder was dirty and muddy. Anything dropping there would have been trampled into the slush.

But it *must* be here, Katie thought. Please, please, let it be here. I can't go home to Mama without the money . . . and without the brooch.

But what if it had fallen up there in the carriage, or out on the track? What if the storm had blown it away? Or if someone else had found it?

No, she mustn't even think such a thought! Katie dropped to her knees. The muddy snow soaked through her skirt and through her petticoat. But Katie hardly noticed. She dug in the snow with her hands, pushing the slush this way and that. People were stepping around her, but Katie paid no attention. When someone stepped on her hand, she hardly even noticed the pain. Her wet gloves were frozen stiff, tears ran down her cheeks—but

Katie went on digging. It had to be here . . . it just had to! But how could one spot a white envelope in the midst of all that white snow?

"Hey, stop crying!" Someone pushed a soggy envelope in front of Katie's face. "Is that what you're looking for?" It was the boy who had helped her down.

"It was right here," the boy said. He pointed to a spot at the foot of the ladder. "You almost buried it with your digging. What's in here, anyway? The way you're carrying on, it must mean a lot to you."

He pushed the envelope into Katie's hands. "Here, you're in my customer's way," he said gruffly. "Better move on."

"Thank you. Thank you so much." Katie could hardly stammer her thanks. She felt like throwing her arms around the boy. How could she show him how grateful she was? All she had to give him was her spare half dime. And he looked as if he could use it too. His jacket was thin and torn. He had rags tied with string around his feet. His gloveless hands looked red.

She held out the coin she had offered him

before. "Please take it," she said. "It's all I can give you to show you my thanks."

But the boy shook his head.

"Don't worry," he said. "I'm making plenty today." He tossed a handful of snow into the air. "Great stuff," he said happily.

Katie smiled at him. "It looks nice," she said, "but I wish it would stop coming down."

But the snow didn't stop. Already the spot where Katie had dug was covered by fresh white drifts. She was beginning to feel the wind again, too. It tore at her shawl, billowed her skirt, pushed against her so that she could hardly walk.

She pushed on, clutching the envelope in her hand. With each step she sank ankle deep into the powdery snow. She hardly felt her feet anymore, but her soggy skirt was turning into a stiff, heavy weight which she had trouble dragging along.

Only five more blocks, Katie thought, to cheer herself. That's not so much. And it *is* only snow.

But even Katie had to admit to herself that

this wasn't "just snow." This was different. There was so much of it . . . mounds and mounds piling up right in the street. And the cold! That icy-cold wind. It seemed to cut right through her coat and shawl and dress. Right through to her very bones.

And the wind almost seemed to have a mind of its own—playing games with her—nasty games—in which she was the loser. Screaming at her, it dodged from side to side, trying to block her way. Whichever way she turned, she couldn't escape its fury. She tried walking backward, she tried hunching over . . . walking bent low like the very old lady who lived on her block. But she couldn't outwit her enemy, the wind—it dodged in and out . . . slapping fistfuls of snow into her eyes until she was blinded by tears, making her chest burn, taking her breath away. Each icy breath seemed to cut her chest like a knife and yet she was gasping for more.

She still walked on. Lots of people were walking . . . right in the middle of the avenue. Everyone had trouble. Some people clung to the pillars of the El to keep from being blown down. Some had put paper bags with eyeholes over their heads to keep the chilly wind from their faces. Others huddled together in doorways for warmth. An old woman staggered and fell, almost disappearing into a snowdrift. A passerby strained to get her back on her feet; then they struggled along together.

Everywhere, carts and wagons were stuck in the snow. Drivers unhitched their horses to lead the tired animals back to the stables. Some even tried to ride their saddleless horses back through the snow. Ahead, a horsecar had been abandoned on its tracks. Some people used the empty carriage as a rest stop. Katie stopped, too. She sank down on one of the wooden benches. What a relief to get out of that gale!

But she couldn't rest long. It must be quite late. Much too late. Mama was home alone with the twins. I must hurry, Katie thought. I must get back home.

On the other side of the street, an uptown trolley was still running. It was so jam-packed with passengers that some nearly spilled out on either end. Others clung to the steps outside, holding on for dear life. The horses strained to pull their load through the snow. Foam bubbled up from their mouths. The driver kept using his whip to make them move on. Katie looked longingly at the passing car. Maybe she should ride back home. She still had the fare.

But I can't give up, Katie thought stubbornly. Not after coming this far.

Katie turned west. One block to Third Avenue. Two or three blocks after that.

On the side street there was no shelter at all from the falling snow. And there was no escape from the wind that shifted about. Sometimes it blew the snow straight into her face, sometimes it pushed from behind. Tall drifts of it blocked her way. Telegraph poles leaned at crazy angles. Some of the wires dipped dangerously close to the ground. Here and there a fallen store sign stuck up out of the piled-up snow.

Another corner to turn. But on Third Ave-

nue things were not any better. More windows shattered by the storm, falling shingles, or blowing debris. More fallen wires, more stranded wagons and carriages blocking the horsecar tracks. And more wind. Always more wind!

Katie counted the cross streets. Forty-sixth Street, Forty-fifth, Forty-fourth . . . Now she really didn't feel her feet anymore, she didn't know how she kept walking. Here was the block she wanted coming up ahead. Now where was that store? It had to be on this street.

She couldn't feel her face anymore either. Katie thought she was crying, but she couldn't feel any tears on her cheeks. She stumbled on. Murray's Grocery Store . . . Mike's Saloon . . . Nathan's Tailoring Establishment.

The sign she wanted hung two houses further down. Three golden balls, the sign for a pawnshop. GOTHAM PAWNSHOP, it said. HARRY LEMMON, PROP.

The window was filled with a jumble of goods: old musical instruments, stacks of plates, glass vases, watches, eyeglasses, rings. . . .

Katie pushed at the door. She rattled the door handle. The door wouldn't budge. It was locked.

Katie peered through the glass. There was no light in the store. It looked dark and empty.

The store was closed! But it couldn't be closed! She had come so far. What about Mama's brooch? Katie couldn't go home empty-handed.

She pounded on the door with both fists. She could hear the noise, but she couldn't feel herself pounding.

"Please, open up," she sobbed. "Please, someone be here!"

But the only answering sound was the rattling of hailstones against the plate-glass windows.

FIVE

The banging went on and on. The noise was hammering in Katie's head. I wish it would stop, she thought.

She was on her knees, leaning against the door. Then the door wasn't there . . . only an open space into darkness. Her hands still stretched out before her, Katie tumbled headlong into the shop.

She lay on the dusty floor, among cardboard boxes and odd bits of bric-a-brac. A man stood over her. He looked very tall.

"What's all this banging?" The voice

seemed to come in uneven waves . . . from far away. "What were you trying to do—break down my door? Couldn't you see we're closed?"

Katie tried to scramble up. But somehow she couldn't quite make it. The pawnshop seemed to spin around her . . . shelves full of ornaments, glass cases crammed with watches and bracelets, racks full of jackets and coats. Hanging lamps and chandeliers filled the ceiling above her.

What banging? Had *she* been banging? The noise had stopped, and that was good. But her thoughts were spinning . . . odd bits of ideas she couldn't hold on to, a fuzzy haze she couldn't quite clear away.

The owner of the shop towered over her. His face floated like a pale disk in the darkness far above her.

Mama's brooch . . . envelope . . . money . . . The bits of thought began to come together in her mind. She was surprised to find that her right hand was still clasped around the envelope—so tightly that she couldn't release her grip. It was even more soiled and tattered now, but it was still sealed. She held it out to the man.

"Here, the money . . . the ticket . . . for Mama's brooch," she gasped.

He took it from her and opened it. She watched him count the money and study the green ticket. Then he looked at her and shook his head in disbelief.

"Hey, Martha," he called. "Come here and see what the storm blew in. Worst storm in years, and we've got a customer. A paying customer."

A woman came in from the room behind the shop, wiping her hands on her apron. She was short and round and gray-haired.

"What's going on?" she asked, peering at Katie through steel-rimmed glasses. "Why, it's a little girl," she cried. She dropped on her knees next to Katie. "Harry Lemmon," she scolded, "this child is half frozen. Can't you see she needs help?"

Katie felt herself being lifted up. Then the fog settled down on her again and for a while she didn't feel anything at all. She had a vague feeling of being undressed. Someone was rubbing her hands and feet. It hurt and she heard herself moaning. There were soothing words—a murmuring of voices.

Then she was sitting at a kitchen table wrapped in a patchwork quilt. Her shoes and stockings were drying in front of an iron stove. There was a delicious spicy smell of cabbage soup. It came from a steaming bowl of broth before her.

"Eat," the pawnbroker's wife urged. "Get something hot inside of you. Poor little thing—those fingers and toes of yours were near to frozen."

Katie wriggled her bare toes. They still tingled some, but at least she could feel her feet again! She wrapped her hands around the warm soup bowl. How hungry she was! She drank the soup greedily, as if she hadn't eaten for days.

The pawnbroker came into the kitchen, carrying Mama's garnet brooch. He put it in Katie's outstretched hand. The graceful little red

bow glistened in the lamplight. It felt so light and it looked so small. But Katie knew that to Mama it meant a great deal. She remembered Mama's wedding picture and the happy look on Mama's face. Maybe Mama would smile like that again when Katie brought home the brooch.

Her hands trembling, Katie pinned the brooch to her old brown dress. She checked to see if it was securely fastened. She mustn't lose it on her way home.

Going home! She'd almost forgotten that she still had to go home. Back out into the storm. It was still snowing. Even in the Lemmons' back kitchen she could hear the wind rattling the shutters outside.

How long had she been here? A tall grandfather clock was ticking away in the corner. Two o'clock! And she had left home before seven. What was happening at home all this time? What if Mama had awakened? She'd be worried . . . or was she too sick to care? And the twins. They must be hungry and scared. I must hurry home, Katie thought.

Her stockings and dress were dry, but her shoes were still damp. Katie tugged at the hard, stiff leather. She could hardly force her feet into those misshapen shoes.

"Wait," Mrs. Lemmon said. She hurried into the shop. She rummaged inside a big box behind the counter.

"Here," she said, handing Katie a pair of dusty old rubber boots. "See if they fit. All the things in this box are unclaimed. If they fit, you can have them."

The boots were big, but Mrs. Lemmon found some heavy woollen stockings in her catch-all box, and a knitted scarf and red-and-white-striped mittens. She tied Katie's own shoes and gloves into a neat parcel.

But when Katie began to put on her coat, Mrs. Lemmon stopped her.

"Not now," she said. "I can't let you go back out into that storm. My Lord, I haven't seen a worse one since the winter of '72! Better wait here until it lets up. Grown men are having trouble today. You'll freeze before you get home."

"I'll make it," Katie insisted. "I have to go home. Mama is sick and the twins are alone. I've been gone too long already."

Mrs. Lemmon shook her head. "No, it's too far," she said firmly. "Nothing is moving out there—see for yourself." She patted Katie on the shoulder. "Cheer up," she said. "I've put the kettle on for a nice cup of tea in front of the warm fire. There, it's whistling now." And leaving Katie in the shop, Mrs. Lemmon hurried back into the kitchen.

Katie stared out through the grimy glass panes of the door. Mrs. Lemmon was right. Nothing was moving on Third Avenue. No vans, no wagons, no horsecars. No railroad trains were shaking the elevated tracks. Only a few people came trudging past, heads bent into the wind. She watched a tall, heavy man stopped by a sudden gust. It looked as if he were wrestling with an invisible opponent. Finally he went on.

One part of Katie wanted to stay. She wanted to be safe and warm and protected in front of that cozy kitchen fire. But something else told her to go. I must try, Katie thought. I must know how Mama is doing. I can't leave her alone any longer. She had been gone so many hours—anything could have happened at home.

Katie touched the brooch, tracing the loops of the bow with her fingers. How pleased Mama would be! Seeing Mama's happy face would be worth everything.

Quickly Katie put on her coat. She wrapped the scarf around her neck and Mama's shawl over her head. From the kitchen she could hear the sound of clinking teacups and the rattle of silverware. The Lemmons were talking to each other, but one of them might come into the shop at any moment and stop her from going.

"I'm sorry, but I *have* to go," Katie whispered. Then she opened the shop door quietly and slipped outside.

SIX

It was even worse than before. It wasn't snow anymore, but tiny icicles—sharp particles that stung her forehead and her cheeks. The sidewalk and street had vanished under soft white mounds in which all car tracks and footmarks had long ago disappeared. Walking through it was like climbing mountains; after just a few steps Katie's legs ached and she was gasping for air.

Another few steps and she knew she couldn't keep walking that way. Her enemy, the wind, had hold of her again—stabbing through her with icy fingers, punching her in the face. It was almost forty blocks to home. Mrs. Lemmon was right. She'd never make it. Never!

She tried going on anyway. But it seemed that each time she took one step forward, the storm pushed her back two. On either side of the street, the wind had whipped the snow into towering snowbanks, six, seven feet tall. Katie sheltered behind one, trying to catch her breath. The snow gave way under her weight like a soft featherbed. It would be nice, Katie thought, to let go, to sink into that downy softness, to close her eyes and rest.

For a moment she did close her eyes. Then someone shook her—hard. A man and a woman were pulling her out of the snowbank.

"You foolish child," the man shouted, "you'll freeze this way. What are you doing out alone in this storm? Don't you know you'll die if you go to sleep in the snow? You must always keep moving."

"I just wanted to rest a minute," Katie mumbled. Her heart pounded with fright.

People sometimes did freeze to death. She had read about it in books. But those things happened out west on the prairies or in the wilderness far north. They didn't happen in New York City, right in the middle of Third Avenue.

"Keep moving," the man told her. "Keep walking until you get home. Don't rest anymore—it's too dangerous out here."

"How far are you going?" the woman asked. "Is your home near? Do you know that the horsecars and trains have stopped running?"

But Katie couldn't answer. "We can't just leave her here, Bill," the woman said. "She'll fall again and freeze. Let's take her home with us till the worst of the storm is over."

Katie didn't protest. She felt numb inside and out. It didn't matter now . . . nothing mattered. . . . She couldn't get home on her own. All she knew was that she couldn't bear to be alone anymore.

And who else would help her? She'd never even make it back to the pawnshop. She was alone in a part of town where she didn't know anyone. She remembered the railroad depot. That wasn't very far away. But Papa wasn't at the depot. He too was somewhere out there in the storm . . . in a stalled train or a faraway town. . . . He didn't even know that Katie wasn't safely home with Mama, that she was wandering around alone. What would Papa tell her to do? Katie wondered. He would tell her to find shelter, Katie was sure.

She let the woman take her by the hand and lead her on.

Even with help each mound of snow seemed harder to climb. Katie lost all sense of direction. Were they still walking uptown? How many blocks? Maybe somewhere there were still horsecars running after all. . . . Meanwhile she just forced her legs to move on—step after step after step.

They turned a corner. Katie could hardly see—her eyes burned from the cold. The snow was so thick, it hung like a screen between her and her new friends. Katie was glad for the comforting touch of the woman's hand on her own.

It took forever to walk the length of the block. The three of them clung together, pulling each other along. Once they barely dodged some falling shingles. Another time a piece of chimney crashed down just behind their backs. Halfway down the block a tangle of telephone wires barred their way. Farther along the sidewalk they had to skirt the broken branches of a fallen tree. At times they moved forward on hands and knees, finding their path by touch. Katie could hear the woman beside her panting with the effort. Her own breath escaped in labored puffs of steam.

Another corner. "Look, we are almost home," the woman said. "I can see the sign of the Windsor Hotel. That's on Forty-seventh Street. Only two more blocks to our house."

Two more blocks. To Katie it sounded like twenty. She stared at the big bulk of the Windsor Hotel. Rows of large, brightly lit windows splashed squares of yellow light onto the snow. How dark it was on the street. Was it night already, or was the storm blotting out all the daylight?

The Windsor Hotel . . . she knew that name. Where had she heard it before? Suddenly Katie remembered. Aunt Maggie! Aunt Maggie worked at the Windsor Hotel! By some strange kind of magic these kind people had led her straight to the one person who would be able to help her.

Katie explained. Suddenly she could talk again.

"Are you sure?" the woman asked. "Can you get to the hotel door by yourself?" Katie was sure. Just knowing that Aunt Maggie was nearby filled her with new strength.

She hugged her new friends. "Thank you. Thank you so much!" Then they were gone— swallowed up in the snowy haze. On her own, Katie fought her way to the door.

She stood just inside the entrance, dripping snow on the marble floor. For a moment the heat and bright lights were almost too much. Katie had to lean against one of the tall marble pillars to keep herself from falling.

No one paid any attention to her. The big high lobby of the Windsor was almost as crowded as a busy railroad depot. Well-dressed people milled about, shoving each other in their haste to get to the desk clerk. Some argued with him. "Please, you must have a room for me," someone pleaded. "Just a bed somewhere, or a cot, to spend the night."

Katie felt timid and strange. All these fancy people. She had never seen so many fur wraps and muffs and fur-collared coats in one place. Maybe she had come in the wrong way. How would she ever find Aunt Maggie in this huge place?

Katie knew she couldn't just stand there. Slowly she walked to the back of the lobby. A man in a splendid uniform stood by the elevator. He gave Katie an icy stare. "Where do you think you're going?" he asked.

Katie wanted to answer, but the words stuck in her throat. Suddenly it was all too much—Mama, and the storm, her long, long walk, her aching hands and feet. . . . She fought her tears, but they welled up anyway, filling her eyes, spilling over. . . .

"Aunt Maggie," she managed to get out. "I'm looking for Maggie Murphy."

The man's eyes softened. Suddenly he wasn't stiff and forbidding anymore. He took Katie by the hand and led her through long back passageways. One flight up they came across a chambermaid, carrying an armful of towels. The maid wore a white apron over a gray dress and a little lace cap on her head.

"Can you find Maggie Murphy for this little lass?" the man asked. "Maggie is her auntie, and she needs her help."

Some more stairs, more long, carpeted hallways. And then Aunt Maggie was there, in the same kind of gray dress and lace cap on her auburn hair. Katie flew into her arms.

And now the tears really came, like a dam giving way. Katie, who never cried . . . Katie, Mama's dependable Kate, crying all over Aunt Maggie's apron until she could hardly cry anymore. And the words came too—between sobs—spilling out in bits and pieces: about Mama's illness and about the brooch, about Papa being away and about the long trip through the snow.

"You foolish child," Aunt Maggie scolded

softly, stroking Katie's hair. "What a chance you took! No brooch in the world is worth taking chances like that." Then she smiled. "But you are safe," she said. "And that's all that counts. Now we'll just have to find a way to get both of us safely uptown."

"But Papa, what about Papa?" Katie asked. Now that she herself was warm and safe, she couldn't bear to think of Papa still out in the storm.

"Your Dad is smart—he knows how to take care of himself." Aunt Maggie laughed.

Once again Katie could feel the warmth spreading through her body. She felt drowsy and content. Everything was all right. She didn't need to worry anymore. Aunt Maggie would take care of everything. She'd take care of Katie—and Mama too. Aunt Maggie would know how to manage.

Katie was so sure about Aunt Maggie that she wasn't even surprised when Aunt Maggie returned with the news that she'd found a way to get them home.

"One of the gentlemen on my floor," she

explained, "has a sleigh waiting outside. He's taking some of his friends to their homes, but he promised to squeeze us in. He's a nice man, Mr. Heatherton is."

Aunt Maggie bustled about. She took off her apron and cap and put on her coat and hat. "Now just a word to the housekeeper," she said, "and then we're off."

"But what if the housekeeper won't let you off?" Katie worried.

"Now don't you worry, my love," Aunt Maggie said. "If she says no, I'll go anyway. Nothing would make me stay, with my own sister so sick and her little ones needing help! There are other jobs."

It was still snowing, but the storm had let up a little when they got outside. The sleigh was waiting. The horses were covered with warm blankets. Aunt Maggie climbed on the driver's seat next to the coachman, but Mr. Heatherton made Katie sit inside the sleigh with him and his friends. He wrapped Katie into a warm lap robe so that nothing showed but her eyes and the tip of her nose.

Even the sleigh horses had a hard time moving through the deep snow. They stopped and strained and they had to rest every few blocks. But Katie was too weary to care. She watched the big houses and streetlamps of Fifth Avenue moving past. She listened to the tinkling of the sleigh bells. She looked up at the trees along Central Park. Some were half down or had lost some of their branches to the storm, but their dark outlines still looked pretty against all that white snow.

Katie wished she could forget her worries for a moment and pretend that this was just a happy outing in a sleigh. She'd never had a sleigh ride like this before! How the twins would enjoy gliding along like this in splendor. She must remember every little detail for them—the sleek horses, the furry lap robe, the stately coachman with his towering high hat.

They stopped at several houses to drop Mr. Heatherton's friends off. At Seventy-ninth Street, Mr. Heatherton got off too.

"William will take you and the child home," he told Aunt Maggie.

"Oh, but we can manage from here, sir," Aunt Maggie protested.

"Nonsense," Mr. Heatherton said. "I have daughters myself. I wouldn't want them trudging about in this storm." He patted Katie on the back. "Take care of yourself, little one," he said.

They turned east. The sleigh crossed the bridge over the open railroad cut on Fourth Avenue. The deep trench was half filled with snow. It would be a while before trains could pass here! Once again Katie thought of Papa. She wondered if he was safe. How would he get home? She hoped he wasn't cold and hungry.

Third Avenue . . . Second Avenue . . . and they were home. Across the street the snow-drifts were piled so high, they almost reached to the second-story windows! But her own side was almost clear. The coachman carried Katie into the house. Aunt Maggie was close behind, her skirt trailing in the snow.

Aunt Maggie helped Katie up the stairs. Katie's fingers and toes had started to hurt again, a dull, throbbing ache. Katie and Aunt Maggie pounded on the door. It was Michael who flung it open. Kevin was right behind him. The Reillys were there, and Mama was propped up in bed.

"Katie, you're safe! Thank God," she cried. She still sounded awfully weak, but she clasped Katie's hand in her own so tightly it felt as if she'd never let it go.

Then Katie gave Mama the brooch. She tired to pin it on Mama's nightgown, but her fingers were too stiff and sore. Aunt Maggie had to help. Mama kept touching the brooch, her eyes shining.

Then Aunt Maggie took charge. She helped Katie undress, as if Katie were no older than Kevin and Michael. She rubbed Katie's throbbing fingers and toes and gently bathed them in lukewarm water. Then she tucked Katie into Papa's side of the bed, next to Mama.

"My two patients." Aunt Maggie laughed. Then she got busy again, scrubbing the twins and fixing supper, freshening Mama's sheets and blankets and tidying all the rooms. In the meantime everyone talked . . . and talked . . . until Katie was nearly hoarse. Over and over, Katie had to tell about her ride on the El, about climbing down the ladder, about fighting the wind and the snow.

"Time to go to sleep," Aunt Maggie said firmly. "Tomorrow is another day." She tucked Katie tightly under her covers. She turned down the kerosene lamp and went to close the curtains.

"It's still snowing," she said.

Warm in bed, Katie felt snug and happy. It felt good to be cozy and safe when the winds howled outside. She wished she could be sure that Papa was safe too. Mr. Reilly had assured her again that trainmen knew what to do in a storm. Yes, Katie thought, Papa was smart. He'd do the right thing and he'd be home as soon as the storm was over. Then they'd talk about their adventures. About being out in the bad storm—the worst storm ever in New York City.

In the dark, she remembered her own day. It had been hard and scary, but she'd done what she'd set out to do. But only because people had helped her. So many kind and nice people: the boy at the ladder, Mr. and Mrs. Lemmon in the pawnshop, the friendly couple on the street, Mr. Heatherton and his sleigh. And, of course, Aunt Maggie.

With a sigh, Katie closed her eyes. She could sleep now because Aunt Maggie was here. Katie turned over and snuggled deeper under her covers.

Perhaps the storm would let up by morning. With Aunt Maggie here to take care of Mama, maybe she and the twins could have fun in the snow.

AUTHOR'S NOTE

The Great Blizzard of 1888 is still remembered as one of the worst weather disasters in the history of New York City. The storm began with rain and sleet on Sunday, March 11. By midnight the rain had turned to snow, and the snow, driven by occasional wind gusts of up to seventy-five miles per hour, continued to cover an unprepared city until early Tuesday morning. While it lasted, twenty inches of snow fell on the city and much of it was swept into snowdrifts, six feet or more, by the relentless winds. Temperatures plunged as low as one degree at times.

New Yorkers, who had enjoyed springlike weather for several weeks, did not realize the dangers of the storm at first. Many tried to get to work as usual on Monday morning. Few made it. The few students who showed up in the city's schools were dismissed early and were told to go home in groups, holding hands all the way. By midday, all traffic had come to a halt. Horsedrawn omnibuses, trolley cars, and cabs bogged down in the deep snow. Frozen switches and blocked railroad tracks prevented trains from entering the city. Ferryboats to and from Brooklyn, Queens, New Jersey, and Staten Island could not operate in the storm. And the fierce winds brought down the telegraph lines, telephone cables, and electric wires on which contact with the outside world depended. The new, and supposedly blizzard-proof, elevated railroads bogged down even earlier than the surface traffic.

Many New Yorkers suffered frostbite or worse that day. Some collapsed and many froze to death in deep snowdrifts. So did many horses.

The Great Blizzard made New Yorkers realize how exposed the city was to weather conditions. Soon afterward, utility cables and wires were moved underground and work was started on the first subway tunnels.

For many years people continued to talk about the hardships they had suffered during the Great Blizzard. As the years passed, "survivors" came together on March 12 to commemorate their adventures. Today, many older people remember stories told by their parents about the events of the day. A few can even remember the blizzard for themselves.

A girl like Katie might well have started out on her errand early that Monday morning, only to run into problems along the way. Without radio, television, telephones, weather satellites, or helicopter weathermen to warn her, she would never have guessed that this wasn't just another late-season snow.